THE
GUN

BALI RAI

To everyone at Barrington Stoke, past and present, for all your support since 2001. Thank you so very much.

www.balirai.co.uk

First published in 2011 in Great Britain by
Barrington Stoke Ltd
18 Walker Street, Edinburgh, EH3 7LP

www.barringtonstoke.co.uk

This edition first published 2015

Text © 2011 Bali Rai

A CIP catalogue record for this book is available
from the British Library upon request

ISBN: 978-1-78112-467-3

Printed in China by Leo

Contents

Prologue

The cell that they held me in stank of sweat. I was in there for two hours before a solicitor turned up. He was someone my mum had rung. Someone who knew my Uncle Clifton, my mum's brother. One of the coppers took me down to an interview room.

"Your solicitor's here," he told me.

"Yeah," I replied.

I walked into the interview room. A middle-aged man was sitting at a table. He was wearing a dark grey suit and a red tie. His hair was dark brown and he wore black and silver D&G glasses. He looked like my science teacher at school –

apart from the expensive frames. The detective who'd arrested me sat at the table too. She was tall and blonde and skinny. She looked up at me.

"Are you ready to tell us what happened?" she asked me.

"Guess," I mumbled.

"OK, take a seat next to your solicitor," she replied. "Can I get you a drink or anything?"

I shrugged.

"I'm OK," I told her. "Can we just get on with it?"

The woman nodded. She looked at the solicitor and then back at me.

"OK," she said. "Tell us what happened. From the start ..."

Chapter 1
Shots

We were down on the High Street, freezing our arses off outside Lahore Fried Chicken, when we heard the gunshots.

Pop! POP POP POP!

Everyone ran as a shiny black Mercedes sped past. I hit the ground hard and my elbow slammed on the pavement. Kamal did the same and then cursed because his jeans got ripped. But Binny didn't move. I thought he was in shock. He just stood there staring at nothing. I could see his breath because it was so cold.

"Get down, you fool!" snapped Kamal. "You wanna get shot or what?"

But Binny didn't reply. He looked down at us and grinned like a nutter. Like he hadn't just heard the gunshots. The staff from the take-away came out and started looking back up the road.

"What they was shooting at?" asked a short, dark-skinned brother with a strong Asian accent.

Binny shrugged and snapped out of his grin. "Some man up by the shops," he replied.

I got up slowly and dusted off my clothes. Then I helped Kamal get up. He was still moaning about his jeans. He moaned all the time, did Kamal, and he had a nasty temper too. Some of the other people from the take-away came out onto the street and a couple of young kids rode up on their bikes. Everyone was trying to work out what had happened.

Suddenly there were two more shots. As everyone took cover, the same black car flashed past again. I watched it go by. At the end of the street, the driver slammed on the brakes. One of the back doors opened and a man ran out, carrying a bag. He went down an alley by the side of the train station. Twenty seconds later he was back in the car. As the police sirens howled in the distance, the black Merc jumped a red light and then it was gone.

"It's getting like cowboy town round here," I said, turning back into the take-away.

Kamal shrugged. "Ain't no big deal," he said. "If them man want to dust each other, let them."

The police were there five minutes later. We watched as they shut off the road around the shops. There were loads of coppers, some with dogs, getting out of cars and vans. And then the armed response units turned up. I watched on, as they started talking to people and scanning the ground for clues.

"I'm gone," I told my mates.

"Me too," replied Binny. I knew he had a little bit of weed on him. "No way I'm chatting to no feds."

Kamal told us that he was going to stick around, to find out what was going on.

"Later," he said, as Binny and I walked out into the street.

"You cutting across the park?" Binny asked.

I shook my head. I wanted to check something but I didn't want Binny to find out.

"Nah – I need to pass by my sister's," I lied.

Once Binny was gone, I walked towards the alley by the station. The one where the gunmen had dumped something. I don't know why I did it. I just wanted to see what they'd left behind. The alley was dark. The only light came from the moon. There was a black rucksack, hidden by some bins. It felt a bit heavy as I picked it up. I opened the bag and looked inside and that was when I found it.

The gun.

Chapter 2
The BMD Crew

When I got home, I ran to my bedroom and locked the door. I lived in a 12th-floor flat with my mum and my younger sister, Hope. I was out of breath because the lifts weren't working. Hope heard me come in and knocked on my door.

"Mind your own business," I said when she asked what I was doing.

Once I knew she'd gone, I opened the bag and lifted the gun out. I did it slowly and carefully. It was black and shiny and felt heavy in my hands. I held it out in front of me and aimed at the window.

"*POW!*" I whispered to myself, then felt like a stupid kid.

I put the gun down on my bed and hunted through the bag. A box of bullets fell out, along with a flick knife.

Next I emptied out the box of bullets. They were gold-coloured and there were ten of them. I held one up and looked at it. It was kind of cool – at least that's what I thought. I looked back at the gun. I couldn't see how it worked. I'd seen people on TV using guns but I knew that wasn't real. And I didn't want to get something wrong and shoot myself or anyone else by accident. I decided to look on the internet to see how the gun worked.

Then my mum knocked on the door.

"Out here now, Jonas!" she said.

"In a minute!" I shouted back.

I stuffed everything back into the bag and pushed it under my bed. When I opened the door my mum gave me a look like she knew I was up to something.

"What's going on?" she asked.

"Nothing," I replied.

She gave me another funny look. She was dressed in a blue nurse's uniform, ready to start her night shift. She looked tired and her brown hair was tied up on her head.

"You had something to eat?" she said.

I nodded in reply. "Got some fried chicken earlier," I said.

"You need to stop eating that stuff," she told me. "It's full of fat."

I smiled at her. "Tastes good, though."

She told me not to make any trouble and then she went off to work. I waited until she was gone before going into the living room. Hope was in there, watching telly. She looked like my mum, with pale brown skin and black freckles across her nose. She had the same light brown curly hair too.

"You're up to summat," she said without looking at me.

"Not me," I said.

My phone, which was in my pocket, started to buzz. I pulled it out and saw that I had a message from Kamal. I didn't have enough credit to call him so I sent a text.

"Who was that?" Hope asked.

"Do I ask you who your mates are?" I asked back.

"You're proper touchy today," she said.

I shrugged. "I'm goin' out for half an hour," I said. "I'll be back quick."

Hope was about to complain but she stopped. I knew she wouldn't tell my mum because I didn't stop her from going out late. We had a deal about keeping our late nights secret.

Hope was a year younger than me, in Year 10 at school. She was like my older sister Lauren, good at school and that. Not like me. I wasn't thick or anything. I just didn't get on with my teachers. I was just killing time until they let me leave.

"You better be back soon," Hope said.

"I will. I'm just going to check Kamal for a bit," I told her.

"That fool," she said as she made a face.

"What's up with Kamal?" I asked her.

"I don't like him," she said. "He's creepy ... like he's always five seconds away from going crazy. And he looks at me funny too. Like he's thinking nasty thoughts."

I gave her a look but didn't reply.

Once I got out of the block of flats, I pulled my grey hood over my head. I was wearing a black beanie hat but my head was still cold. The wind was strong, freezing my nose and cheeks. My teeth were almost chattering. It took me ten minutes to get to Kamal, down by the estate next to ours. He was waiting in the darkness, round the corner from a row of shops.

"They're sitting on a wall," Kamal told me when I got there.

He was like a ghost looming out of the shadows. He had a black puffa jacket on over a white hoodie and he'd changed out of his ripped jeans and had some different ones on. They were black too. I looked at him and thought about what my sister had said. He was a bit weird but he wasn't that bad. Not like Hope had made out.

"Opposite the off-licence – five of dem," he added.

Kamal was talking about a crew from the next estate who'd jumped Binny and him a week before. They were called the Blakemore Massive Dem after the name of their estate. The BMD Crew. Me and Binny wanted to forget about it, but Kamal wasn't having it. He told us we'd lost face and people were calling us pussies.

"Them man can't just walk around like they ain't done nothin'," he'd said. "We need some respec' – you get me?"

Now we were standing round the corner from them, on their estate. It wasn't a good place to be. And I could see on Kamal's face that he was about to run some madness.

"Come," I said to Kamal. "Let's leave it for some other time."

Kamal shook his head.

"Forget that," he spat. "Them man are laughin' at us."

He walked to the corner and looked round slowly. Then, without warning, he pulled something from his jacket. Before I could stop him he ran towards the BMD crew.

I cursed to myself. But I knew I had to follow him. He was my mate and if you didn't back up your mates, you weren't nothing.

When I got to Kamal he was holding off two lads with a small blade. They were both older than us and big too, but the shiny knife in Kamal's hand stopped them doing anything. The rest of their crew must have run away. I jumped the lad nearest to me and punched him in the side of the head. He cried out but then he started fighting back. I caught a fist right on my nose and my eyes started to water.

We'd been fighting for a couple of minutes when the rest of their crew came back. I heard a "BMD" shout go up and saw another five lads running towards us, waving baseball bats.

"RUN!" I shouted at Kamal. We were in trouble now.

I span round and sprinted back to the corner and then across a little park, to the road that ran between the two estates. Kamal was right behind me and, a little way off, still running after us, were the other crew.

I ran across the busy road, dodging cars, and on towards the High Street. Kamal was just behind me still. My lungs were burning with the effort but I knew that if we made the High Street we'd be safe. It was crawling with police because of the shooting.

I was right. As soon as me and Kamal reached the High Street, the BMD crew stopped chasing us. I turned to face them as Kamal started to cough.

"Come on, then!" I shouted. I knew they'd stop there. They weren't stupid enough to fight on a street packed with police.

They turned and ran off. Kamal watched them go and started cursing.

"Nah!" he shouted. "We was supposed to run them off!"

I rubbed my hands together to warm them up. The sweat on my face had already started to freeze.

"Forget it, bro," I told him. "They would have battered us."

"So?" Kamal asked, his dark eyes shining with anger. He was snarling at me, like a crazy dog would.

Kamal was always angry. Ever since he was little he'd been fighting people and getting into trouble. I'd known him longer than anyone and even I didn't know why.

Everyone I knew was poor, but Kamal's family were refugees when they first came to England and they had it *proper* hard. For years Kamal had to wear second-hand clothes from the charity shop. The other kids would rip him over it. And he'd get even by beating them up. Then his old man got stabbed to death by some racist white bwoy and things had got even worse. Kamal was like my brother but even I couldn't control the man. No one could.

I should never have told him about the gun – I know that now. But how was I supposed to know back then? I didn't know what he'd do, did I?

Chapter 3
Standing up to Them

The next week, the cops were everywhere I went. They were all over our estate looking for clues. The guys in the Merc had killed someone, so now the police were running a murder enquiry. We all knew the person they'd shot. His name was Johnny Charles and he was about three years older than us. He was a street player – a drug dealer and loan shark – that no one liked too much. He was a bully who'd pick on the younger kids and give people he didn't like a hard time.

The police had real trouble getting anyone to talk to them. It's like that round here. No one trusts the feds. By the end of the first week, the murder made the national news and the police were asking for witnesses. Part of me wanted to tell them about the gun but I didn't. I kept the gun and said nothing. It was stupid and wrong and I'm ashamed of it but back then, when it happened, I wasn't thinking straight.

I told Binny about the gun first, one week after the murder. We'd had some more trouble with the Blakemore Massive Dem crew. Binny, me and some other lads had been kicking a football around on a patch of grass. The BMD jumped us and we had to run. There were about 20 of them, all tooled up. Me and Binny only just made it to my mum's flat.

"That was close," said Binny, as I closed the front door, praying the gang hadn't seen us.

"This ain't right," I told him. "Someone's gonna get hurt."

Binny was my oldest friend, other than Kamal. We'd lived next door to each other for years. Then Binny's mum and dad split up. Binny and his mum moved to another tower block but it wasn't far from us. He was tall and thin with curly black hair like his dad, who was from Morocco, but he had blue eyes like his mum who was white. The girls all loved Binny like he was some celebrity and he always had one on the go. He was a proper playa.

"They got numbers on us," Binny said, taking a seat on the sofa.

I turned the telly on and sat down next to him. I put my feet up on the small table in front of us.

"Yeah – there must be 20 of them at least," I replied.

We didn't have a name for our crew – not a proper one anyway. Our estate was called the Dunsmore Gardens so some of the youths called themselves the Dunsmore Bad Bwoy or DBB. But me, Binny and Kamal weren't really into that too much.

"So how we gonna stand up to them?" Binny asked. He'd grabbed the remote and now he was flicking through the channels.

I shrugged. "I might have a way," I said. That was my first mistake.

See, if I'd just told Binny about the gun and no one else, things would have been fine. But I couldn't tell Binny and not Kamal. That would have been bad. We were brothers, the three of us. We didn't have any secrets. In my head I was thinking we could just use the gun for protection.

"What way?" asked Binny. He turned to look at me.

"I found summat, bro," I said. "After the shooting on the High Street."

Binny put down the remote.

"What?" he asked.

I got up and went to my room. I came back with the bag and dropped it on the sofa.

"Open it," I said.

"Why – what's in the bag?" Binny gave me a funny look.

"Man – just open and see," I replied.

He looked at me for a few more seconds and then did what I told him.

"What the ...!" he began but he couldn't finish his sentence. He lifted the gun and looked at it with big wide eyes. "Where'd you get this?" he asked me.

"The night Johnny Charles got killed. I seen the gunmen throw it in the alley."

He gave me another funny look. "Why would they throw it away?" he asked.

"I dunno, do I?" I said. "But I grabbed it before the police could get it."

Binny shook his head.

"This is the *murder* weapon, bro. The ting they been askin' about on the news," he said.

I nodded.

"We get catch with this ting ..." he added, then he shook his head again.

"No one knows we've got it," I pointed out. "And we ain't telling no one either."

Binny looked at the gun again. He held it out in front of him, aiming at the telly.

"Is it loaded?" he asked me.

"I dunno, bro. I ain't never used no gun before, have I?"

He let out a soft whistle, like he was impressed.

"We can use it to make them BMD pussies back off," I said.

Binny shook his head. "I ain't about to shoot no man," he told me. "Not unless they try to kill me."

"We don't have to shoot anyone," I replied. "We just scare them – nothing else. Once they know we've got this they'll back off anyway, bro."

Binny thought about it for a minute and then he shrugged. "What else is in the bag?" he asked, as he looked inside.

I thought about the money and I nearly told him but before I could, someone started banging on the door. I grabbed the gun from Binny.

"You think they saw us come in here?" I whispered to him.

"Nah, man," he said.

"Let me go check," I replied. I took the gun with me.

My mum was at work and Hope was at her boyfriend's house so I knew it wasn't them at the door. I walked slowly down the hall. The person at the door started banging even louder.

"Come on – let me in, bro!" he shouted.

I gave a sigh and put the gun in my back pocket. It was Kamal at the door. When I opened it, he was grinning at me.

"You crap the bed or summat?" he asked. "You look well para."

I shook my head.

"I heard about the BMD from someone at the chicken shop," he added.

I told him to come in and he went into the living room. I checked the landing outside the flat before I went in too. I needed to make sure no one else was watching or anything. When I got to the living room, Kamal was sitting next to the bag, with the box of bullets in his hand.

"Where'd you get this?" he asked. His eyes were wide open and shining.

I told Kamal how I'd found the gun. Then we spent a couple of hours playing FIFA on my Nintendo Wii and pretending to be gangsters. We took turns holding the gun and pointing it at each other. We were like kids playing with a new toy. By the time Binny and Kamal left, it was two in the morning.

"Best let me have the shooter," said Kamal when he got to the front door.

"Why?" I asked him.

"You're already in your yard," he replied. "Me and Binny gotta walk across the estate still. Them BMD man might be out there."

I thought about it and nodded.

"Take it," I said, "but bring it back tomorrow, bro. We'll hide it in my room."

Kamal looked like he didn't understand. "Why d'you want it back?" he asked.

"Because I found it," I said. "Besides, your yard is full of people. There's only three of us in here. Less chance of being caught."

Kamal thought about what I'd said for a moment and then he grinned at me. "True, true," he replied.

I went back to the living room and got the gun. But I didn't give it to Kamal. I handed it to Binny. I didn't think it was a big deal. I was wrong.

Chapter 4

Ambush

The madness didn't start straight away. For about a week things were OK. Kamal brought the gun back. I knew he'd have got it off Binny. I hid it back under my bed, behind an old suitcase and stuff. One morning we took a trip to the library, planning to go into school late.

The staff in there gave us dirty looks but the internet was free and we didn't bother anyone. I told Binny and Kamal to take down their hoods so that we wouldn't get some oldie spying on us.

We took one computer between us and started looking up stuff to do with guns. It didn't take us long to find a website that told us all we needed to know. It had a video clip on it, showing how to load and unload a gun like ours. The man on the video, some old American guy, even showed how to clean the thing. He called the gun a revolver because of the barrel which you could spin round. The barrel held six bullets. By the time we were done, we knew exactly how it worked.

I went up to school for lunchtime and told Binny and Kamal to come over late, after my mum had gone to work.

Binny turned up first, just after my mum had left. He was so early he must have passed her on the stairs. My sister looked well happy to see him, too. She led him into the living room where I was watching some reality TV show about cops with cameras.

"You're early," I said to him. Hope was grinning like a cat.

"I was bored," he replied and sat down next to me. "I was gonna hang out on the High Street but it's colder than the North Pole out there, bro."

"You want a drink or summat?" Hope asked him.

"I'm OK," he told her, letting her have one of his smiles that the girls all love.

"Yo!" I joked. "That's my sister ... leave it out."

Hope gave me a dirty look and went off to her own room.

We chatted about some other stuff for a while before Kamal showed up. He looked angry and I could see someone had just hit him round the face.

"What happened to you?" I asked.

"Two of them jumped me," he replied. "Came out of nowhere. Abu, the man from the chicken shop, ran them off."

"This is getting stupid now," said Binny.

Kamal looked at me. "Time to give them BMD man a warning," he said. "We'll take the gun. You up for it?"

I wanted to say no but I couldn't let him down. The problem with where we live is that you have to represent. If you don't stand up, you get knocked down. That was just the way things went. I looked at Binny and back to Kamal.

"Come," I said. "But we ain't shooting no one, you get me?"

Kamal grinned.

"Hey, Jonas, I ain't no murderer," he replied. "We're just gonna give them a warning."

We decided to ambush the BMD crew at the shops where Kamal and I had the fight two weeks back. We hid in the alley behind the shops and waited. It was dark down there. No one was around but we knew that some of them would turn up sometime. It was freezing cold and it began to rain softly. We were on the Blakemore Estate – *their* territory – and I started to get worried. I could see things going wrong for us. And Kamal was in a serious mood.

"When they turn up," he whispered to me and Binny, "let me do the talking."

"Whatever, bro," Binny replied.

"What are you gonna say?" I asked.

"Dunno – but them man need to know they can't mess with us, you get me?"

"What if they don't listen?" I added.

Kamal looked at me and I could see the anger in his eyes. He'd got the gun and it was in his jacket pocket. He patted it.

"They'll listen, bro," he said. "Trust me." He sounded evil.

For the next ten minutes we waited in silence, getting colder and colder. My nose was running and the rain was soaking through my hoodie. Even my feet had started to freeze.

"It's cold as –" I began.

"Ssshh!" whispered Kamal. "Someone's coming."

We were standing behind some big bins but we could see past them to the street. There were three lads walking towards the shops and they were definitely BMD. Kamal pulled the string on his hoodie tight.

"Come ...!" he whispered.

He crept past the bins slowly, with me and Binny behind him. The BMD crew went into a fried chicken shop. I pulled Kamal to one side. "We can get them when they come out of the shop," I said.

But Kamal wasn't listening. He walked straight into the shop and pulled out the gun.

"*GET DOWN!*" Kamal shouted.

Binny went in after him and I stood by the door, just in case anyone else turned up. The shop staff stopped what they were doing and put their hands up. Kamal was in the middle of the shop, holding the gun in front of him. The three BMD lads were the only other people in there. Kamal pointed the gun at them.

"Get on the floor!" he shouted.

Two of the lads did as they were told. But the third one stayed where he was. The men behind the counter didn't move.

"You want me to shoot you?" Kamal asked the lad who was still standing.

"Do what you like," the lad replied.

"Down! NOW!" Kamal yelled.

The BMD lad still didn't move so Kamal aimed the gun straight at his head.

"I'm gonna count to three," he said softly. "One ... two ..."

One of the other lads grabbed his mate and pulled him down.

"Don't be a fool," I heard him say. "He's got a shooter."

When all three lads were on the floor, Kamal walked over to them. He held the gun at the head of the third lad.

"Stay away from the Dunsmore," he warned. "Or next time you get a bullet."

No one said anything for a moment. I looked up and down the street. There was no one coming but I was still nervous.

"Come!" I shouted. "Let's jet."

"Yeah," Binny added. "Time to move, bro."

Kamal told us to hold on. He walked to the counter and pointed the gun at one of the staff.

"Money," he snapped.

I looked at Binny. That wasn't in the plan. I kept my mouth shut. What could I say? The man behind the counter scowled at Kamal but he opened the till and pulled out all the cash.

"Put it in one of them paper bags," Kamal told him. "And give me 12 spicy wings too."

This time Binny gave me a look. He didn't need to say anything. What the hell was Kamal up to?'

"Hurry up!" I warned.

Kamal took the money and the wings and turned to us. He had a big grin on his face. I stepped out of the door, with Binny behind me. We stood outside and waited for Kamal. But when he got to the door he turned round.

"Just in case you think I'm blagging," he said. "DBB run tings!"

And then he fired a shot at the ceiling.

The sound was deafening and one of the BMD crew moaned softly. But I didn't have time to ask Kamal what he was doing. As soon as he fired the shot, Kamal ran past me and Binny. He was laughing like a nutter, holding the gun down to his side. Me and Binny ran after him, back through the alley and out of the estate. We didn't stop running until we got to the road.

Kamal put the gun away and walked slowly back across the road. We heard a police siren. I caught up with Kamal on the other side of the road and we turned into the High Street.

"What was that about?" I asked him.

"What?" he replied. "I didn't do nothing."

He grinned and began to eat a chicken wing, spitting the bones out as we walked.

"No one said nuttin' about no robbery," Binny said. "You could have got us nicked."

"Chill, bro," Kamal replied. "Ain't no big thing."

It took another ten minutes to get to our estate and no one spoke in that time. I was so angry with Kamal that I couldn't speak. I couldn't believe what he'd done. When we got to the tower blocks, I turned to go home.

"Check you later," I said to the other two.

Binny nodded but Kamal looked pissed off.

"What's up wit' you?" he asked me.

"Nothing," I replied. "Give me the gun."

Kamal shook his head.

"I'll drop it by tomorrow," he said, but I could tell he didn't mean it.

I was going to say something but Kamal looked right at me. And his eyes were set like black stones. I'd never thought of my best mate as scary before.

Chapter 5
Gun Crazy

On Saturday I slept in all morning. And when I got up, my bedroom was even colder than normal. I pulled the brown curtains to one side and looked out. All over the city was a thin cover of snow. I groaned and thought about going back to bed. And then my phone beeped. I grabbed it and read a text from Kamal. I hadn't seen him since we'd robbed the chicken shop on the Blakemore. And he hadn't given me the gun back.

Twenty minutes later I was outside Lahore Fried Chicken, stamping my feet to keep them warm and watching the world go by. Kamal had told me to meet him there but he was late. In the end I went into the shop. It was too cold to hang around outside. The owner, Abu, was at the counter and he was talking in some Asian language to one of the staff. Abu looked really angry.

"Something up, bro?" I asked him, when he looked at me.

"My cousin-brother shop get robbed," replied Abu and shook his head.

Something happened inside my stomach. I looked away from Abu. "Where's his shop?" I asked. I was praying he couldn't see the panic on my face.

"Blakemore," Abu said.

He was talking about the shop that we'd robbed.

"Is your cousin OK?" I added quickly, trying to relax.

Abu shrugged. "OK – but they use gun. Now his shop closed until he fix the damage," he told me.

"That's bad, bruv," I said.

For a moment I thought he knew that we'd done it. But I was wrong. After a few seconds Abu grinned at me.

"You have some spicy chicken – keep warm then, innit?"

"Nah," I said. "I ain't even had no breakfast yet."

But Abu didn't listen. Instead he made me a chicken burger and put it on the counter.

"You pay some other time," he said to me.

I took the food, said thank you and walked out of the shop. I was feeling really bad about his cousin and what we'd done to his shop. But then Kamal turned up. He was humming to himself and looking pleased.

"What you smiling at?" I asked him.

"Got us some more money," he replied.

"Where from?" But in my heart I knew what he'd done. He'd robbed someone else. I could feel it.

"Forget where," he told me. "And best you don't know anyway."

I walked up close to Kamal and whispered my reply. "You're gonna get us nicked. You can't just use the gun for –"

Kamal shook his head before I could finish. "You're going soft," he told me.

"The take-away you robbed the other day belongs to Abu's cousin," I said. "He was talking about it."

"So?" Kamal asked. "He don't know it was us, does he?"

"Not yet he don't," I said. "But the way you're goin' on – acting all mad an' that – it's only a matter of time, bro. You can't be doin' them tings."

"I can do what I like, and you need to watch how you speak to a man."

Kamal didn't shout but I was still scared. It was the way he'd looked at me – like I wasn't there. He didn't even blink. His eyes were shiny and he looked a bit mad.

"Whatever," I replied. No way was he going to know I was worried.

I knew Kamal was going to keep the gun. He wasn't ever going to give it back. And there was nothing I could do about it. My sister had warned me about him. What was it she'd said – that he was always five seconds from going crazy? She'd been right.

"Come," he said and suddenly he snapped into a better mood. "Let's go up town. I'm paying."

I wanted to say no but I couldn't. It was like I didn't want to upset him. I told him I'd text Binny.

"He should come too," I said.

"True," replied Kamal.

I sent Binny a text and then, to kill even more time, I started eating my chicken burger.

"Let me get some too," said Kamal. "Anything to get out of this weather, bro – you get me?"

I shrugged and went back inside the shop with Kamal.

We met Binny in town and spent the rest of the day just walking around. We spent as much time in the shops as we could, looking at clothes and trainers. We needed to stay warm. Kamal had a lot of money with him. But I didn't ask him about it and neither did Binny. And, anyway, he got us both a McDonald's and a load of other stuff too. I did want to know. I was just too scared of him to ask.

I didn't get a chance to speak to Binny on his own until we got to Foot Locker. Kamal went up to the first floor on his own and I tapped Binny on the back.

"He robbed somewhere else this morning," I told him in a whisper.

Binny nodded.

"I guessed that, bro," he replied. "And he's goin' on like a fool too, splashing the money round. Did you see the look we got in Top Man when he pulled out that fat bunch of notes?"

This time I nodded. "We're gonna get caught out," I said. "I can see it happening."

Binny shrugged. "Maybe we should talk to him?" he said.

"I tried that earlier, Binny," I told him. "And the man about warned me off."

Binny looked at me like he didn't believe me.

I told him about what happened outside Lahore Fried Chicken. By the time I was done, Binny was shaking his head.

"He's gone crazy, blood," he said.

"I know," I replied. "But what are we gonna do about it? He's the one with the gun."

"Yeah," said Binny. "And if he's got the gun – he's got all the power too."

I hadn't thought about it like that. Binny was right. There was no way we could stop Kamal if he had the gun. It did give him power. I couldn't believe how quickly he'd flipped. Like, one minute he was a brother to us. And the next minute he was acting like he ruled over us. And I knew that if we tried to stop him, he'd turn on us.

"I just wanna get home," Binny said.

"WHY?" I heard a voice say behind us.

We turned to see Kamal looking right at us. I didn't know what to say, but Binny blagged it.

"Just cold, bro," he said quickly. "It's like penguin heaven outside."

For a moment Kamal just looked at us but then he broke into a grin, like nothing was going on. Binny and me did the same.

"One more stop," Kamal told us, "and then we'll head back."

I nodded. "Where we going?" I said.

"Don't ask," Kamal replied, with a sneering smile. "Just follow, bro. It's me who runs tings now, you get me?"

Kamal took us to a railway bridge. On one side was our estate and the High Street. On the other side was the Blakemore. The bridge had been closed for repairs and there were danger signs everywhere. But Kamal ignored them. He pulled the fences to one side so we could get onto the bridge. Then we crossed over to the Blakemore side. The cold wind was making us shiver and snow had started to fall again too. It was dark.

"What are we doing here?" I asked Kamal.

"Some of them BMD man walk past here," he told us.

"But we ran them last week," Binny reminded him. "After that gun went off they ain't gonna come back for us."

Kamal shook his head.

"It's like them video games," he told us. "When I play *Resident Evil* I look for all the zombies. Even the ones that ain't chasing me."

I looked over at Binny. He gave me the same look back. What the hell was Kamal talking about?

"But ..." I began, but Kamal stopped me. He took out the gun and pointed it straight at me. My heart started thumping in my chest and I couldn't hear properly.

"You don't get it," he said to me, holding the gun still.

"Put that ting down, bro," I heard Binny shout.

"I ain't gonna shoot," Kamal replied. "I'm just makin' a point, bro."

This time he turned and aimed at Binny.

"*Kamal!*" I shouted.

"You and Jonas are weak," he said to Binny. His eyes were glassy and dead-looking. He was like a madman. "It's down to me to earn us respect."

"What respect?" I asked. "What are you on about?"

"From them, man," replied Kamal. "The BMD, the feds, them teachers at school. And I'm sick of being the poor one all the time. There's pure money out there, bro. You just have to take it."

He was babbling. That was the moment when I knew things were badly wrong. Kamal really had gone crazy – *gun* crazy. It was the beginning of the end.

I heard some voices coming from the Blakemore side of the bridge. Kamal heard them too.

"See?" he snapped. "I told you there are always more zombies!"

Before we could do anything he pointed the gun into the darkness. And then, without looking or aiming, he started to shoot.

I grabbed Binny by the arm and we ran for it.

Chapter 6
Trapped

We didn't stop running until we reached my block. As soon as we were in my mum's flat, I bolted the door shut.

"He's gonna kill someone," I said to Binny.

"I know. What are we gonna do?"

We went into the living room and sat down on the sofa. The flat was empty. My sister had gone to stay with a friend and Mum was working. If either of them had seen how scared me and Binny were, they'd have asked lots of questions, so it was good they were out.

What could we tell them anyway? That our best mate had gone mental? That I'd given him a loaded gun? Things were bad enough without my mum shouting at me too.

"We can't do jack," I said to Binny. "He won't give us the gun. And I'm not going to ask him for it."

"What if we tell someone?" asked Binny.

"Like who?" I replied.

When I saw Binny look down, I understood what he meant.

"The *police*?" I asked.

Binny shrugged.

"Can't see what else," he replied.

"But we don't talk to the feds," I told him.

Binny sat back on the sofa and sighed. "This ain't *Resident Evil*, Jonas. There ain't no extra lives in this game!" he told me. "What if Kamal does kill someone? Like what if he shoots a *kid* or something?"

Binny had a point. How bad would I feel if Kamal killed someone? It would all be down to me. I was the one who took the gun. I was the one who'd kept it. And I was the one who'd told Kamal all about it. If someone died, it would be my fault. I thought some more, then I told Binny he was right.

"OK then," I said. "But Kamal must never know, got it?"

Binny nodded. "I ain't gonna tell him," he said. "Kamal is all twisted up in his head."

"If he finds out about this we're dead," I added.

There was a police station on the estate. After we'd had a cup of tea to get warm, Binny and I got up to go. But when I opened the door, I knew something was wrong. I looked down the landing and saw someone standing in the shadows. At first I thought it was the BMD crew, out for revenge. But then I saw Kamal's clothes and trainers.

"What you doin', bro?" I asked him.

But Kamal didn't reply. He just stood in the darkness watching me and Binny.

"This ain't right," Binny whispered to me.

"I know," I replied just as softly.

Suddenly Kamal started laughing. He was like someone out of a horror film. It was a laugh but not a nice one. I backed into Binny.

"Inside," I whispered.

"But ..." Binny began.

I didn't wait for him to finish. I pushed him into the flat and slammed the door shut. A few moments later a shadow fell across the glass on the front door. It was Kamal. He knocked on the door softly.

"What?" I shouted. "What do you want?"

Kamal didn't say anything. He just stood at the door and knocked again, softly. He went on knocking for about a minute and then he stepped back. I saw him lift his arm and I knew what he was going to do. I hit the ground and waited for the bullet to smash through the door.

But nothing happened. Instead Kamal started to hum something. I crawled into the living room where Binny was waiting.

"Kamal's outside," I told him. "We're trapped!"

Binny was scared. His face had gone grey and was damp with sweat.

"But we ain't done nothing to him," he whispered.

"I know, but he's not right in the head," I replied. "He's gone mental."

"What we going to do?"

I didn't have an answer for Binny. I had no clue what to do. Everything felt weird. Kamal was our mate. We'd grown up together. But the gun had changed all of that. One minute things had been fine, like normal. And the next we were hiding in my mum's flat, with Kamal trying to freak us out. It was like being in a nightmare. Only it was much, much more scary.

Kamal left around midnight – I didn't know the exact time. Binny and me had stayed in the living room, trying to stay cool. Every now and then I'd checked to see if Kamal was still at the door. He always was – I could see his shadow – but then, after what seemed like ages, he left.

"I have to get home," said Binny.

"OK," I said.

But Binny didn't move. He just sat and looked at me. At last I worked out what was wrong with him.

"I'll come with you," I told him. "Up until your block."

"Thanks, Jonas," he said.

We didn't see Kamal anywhere as we walked over to Binny's block of flats, but it wasn't far.

On the way back I started to feel scared again. I hadn't thought about walking back on my own. Kamal could ambush me at any time. Underpasses ran all over our estate and every time I passed one, my heart started beating fast. What if he was waiting for me?

I started walking faster, pulling my hood right down and keeping my hands out of my pockets. There were people around, mostly older lads and a few drug dealers.

But I didn't see Kamal. Not until I got to the landing of my mum's flat. For some reason I looked back down into the estate. Down in the car park, I saw Kamal. He was robbing someone at gun point. I kept on watching. The person he was robbing lay flat on the ground. Suddenly Kamal looked up, right at me. I pulled back, praying that he hadn't seen my face. Then I went back into the flat and locked the door.

Chapter 7

Hope

After that night, Kamal vanished. No one saw him on the Sunday at all. Me and Binny kept indoors. When we did go out for a bit, we stayed on the Dunsmore with some other lads. We were going to talk to the police after the weekend.

But by Sunday night, Kamal's family were looking for him. His mum even knocked on our door to ask if I'd seen him. When I said no, she started to cry and my mum asked her in for a cup of tea. One of Kamal's brothers, Yanik, asked me the same thing when I stepped out of the flat. He walked over to the stairs with me and we sat down. It was snowing again and the wind was freezing but I didn't want to be in the flat.

"He didn't come home last night," Yanik told me.

"I ain't seen him since we went into town yesterday," I replied.

"Even when he's late, he always comes back," Yanik said and he pulled his red hoodie over his head.

"I dunno what to tell you," I said, looking away.

Yanik coughed and then pulled some fags from his pocket. "You want one?" he asked, after lighting up his own.

I shook my head.

"Thing is," he said, "I was chattin' to some man down by the High Street. They told me about some trouble with the BMD crew."

I nodded. There was no point saying I didn't know about it. Everyone on our estate got trouble from the BMD.

"We sorted that," I said.

"My uncles want to go to the Blakemore – ask around about Kamal ..."

I shrugged. "Could be an idea," I said. "Have you told the police?"

Yanik nodded. "First thing my mum did. But they weren't bothered."

I wanted to tell Yanik about the gun but I held back. Maybe I felt bad about it. Or maybe it was because I didn't want to tell him that his brother had gone crazy. We chatted some more and then his mum came out and they left together. I walked back into the flat. I knew that my mum would want some answers now.

"Do you know where he is?" she said, as soon as I walked in.

"No," I replied. "He went off yesterday and I ain't seen him since."

My mum looked right into my eyes. "If he's in trouble you can tell me," she said.

"I dunno about no trouble," I lied. "Maybe he's just gone off or summat."

She sighed and went into the kitchen.

Kamal didn't show up on Monday either. By the time I met Binny it was dark again and everyone was asking about our friend.

"He got in trouble?" asked Abu at the fried chicken shop.

"Nah," said Binny. "Nuttin' like that, bro."

But the look on Binny's face said something else. And Abu saw.

"You need my help," he said to us, "just ask me."

I nodded. "Thanks, bro."

We got some food and went back to Binny's. Neither of us said anything about going to the police. Like we'd just made up our minds to forget about it. But we were hiding from the problem and that never works.

Just after 10 p.m. my mobile beeped. It was my sister. I left my phone in my pocket and told Binny to hook up his PlayStation. But then my phone beeped again. And again.

I pulled it out. All three texts were from my sister. Something was wrong. My heart nearly stopped.

"NO!" I shouted.

"What's up?" asked Binny, looking up from the PlayStation.

"Kamal's with Hope!" I shouted. "And he's giving her a hard time. Come on!"

Binny grabbed his jacket. We ran out of his flat and into the estate. Some of the other youths saw us running and came with us. By the time we got to my block I was out of breath and my chest was hurting. I had to get to my sister.

I slammed the doors at the bottom of the stairs open, almost knocking a couple of people over. I didn't have time to apologise. I ran up as fast as I could. My legs were burning. When I got to my floor, I slowed down. I didn't want to run straight into Kamal and the gun. Music was playing in one of the other flats. The bass line was loud and heavy. The landing light had been smashed again.

I walked slowly out onto the landing, with Binny right behind me. The wind was like ice, freezing the sweat on my face. We were 12 floors up. I looked over the landing wall and saw that a crowd of youths had gathered. They were pointing in our direction. Binny whispered, "What now?"

I pointed to the door of my mum's flat.

"We go in," I said.

"What if Kamal is in there?" Binny asked.

"Hope is in there," I told him. "That's all I care about."

The door to the flat was open but there were no lights on. I knew that Hope was home because of the texts she'd sent me. I pushed the door and stepped inside. I could hear a sound coming from the living room. Someone was crying. Hope!

I slammed the door open and found her. She was lying on the floor and her mouth was bleeding. I helped her up and asked her what had happened.

"Kamal," she croaked. "He was looking for you. He had a gun."

I hugged my sister. Then I asked her where Kamal had gone.

"I told him to get lost and he punched me," she replied. "Then he ran off. He said he was going to kill you … and then come back for me."

I could feel myself getting more and more angry. It didn't matter what was going on between me and Kamal. He shouldn't have hit my sister. I was so angry I wanted to strangle him. I turned to Binny, ready to go after Kamal.

But I didn't have to go after him. The door fell open. There was Kamal, standing in the dark. Holding the gun.

He was pointing the gun straight at me.

Chapter 8

Angry

"I ain't never liked you," Kamal said.

He spat the words out like they were poison. I stared back at him. Part of me was scared because of the gun. But mostly I was angry. So angry that I didn't think. I charged at him, crashing past Binny. Kamal didn't have time to react. I was on him in a flash. We started to fight. The gun fell from his hands. Then we hit the hall floor and rolled towards the front door. I had to get him outside. But Kamal was just as strong as me. Every time I thought I had control of him, he broke free.

Suddenly he had his hands around my throat. He started to squeeze his hands together. I began to feel dizzy. My head was going light. I was choking and coughing. I knew that if I didn't do something he'd strangle me to death.

I reached down to one of my pockets. I had a pen there. I pulled it out and stabbed Kamal in the leg. He groaned in pain and let go of my throat. I rolled over and tried to suck in some air. I felt like I was going to puke.

Kamal got up on his knees and began to crawl towards the gun. But I didn't let him. I jumped up and grabbed him. Then I started to drag him out of the door. That was all I could think of. Get him outside! Get him outside!

We crashed onto the landing and started to fight again. Kamal threw some wild punches at my head and I ducked them. I drove a solid fist into his belly. It caught his ribs and made him gasp. I hit him again. He bent over double, coughing like one of them old smokers. I charged him.

Kamal hit the landing wall, with me right behind him. The impact must have hurt him badly because he screamed. And then he tried to get his hands round my throat again. I didn't let him. Just as he stood up, I pushed into him, shoving him as hard as I could. His back hit the landing wall and for a split second he was balancing on the edge ...

And then, as I heard my sister scream, Kamal slipped and fell over the landing.

A second later there was a loud thud. I rushed to the landing and looked over the broken wall. Kamal was lying on the ground, 12 floors down. He wasn't moving.

Epilogue

The solicitor looked at me.

"Is that all there is?" he said.

"Yeah," I replied.

"Are you sure, Jonas? There isn't anything you're hiding?" added the detective.

I shook my head.

"OK, then," she said, and she closed the notebook she'd been writing in.

"What now?" I asked.

The detective shrugged.

"There's a minimum sentence for possession of a firearm," she told me. "And there's the charge for what happened to Kamal. The CPS is looking at it – could be manslaughter. To be honest, Jonas, I just don't know what'll happen. But the fact that you've been straight with us will help. And you have witnesses too."

I looked at my solicitor.

"What do you think?" I asked him.

"Detective Brown is right," he said, smiling at me. "We'll talk about this at our next meeting. After court."

I nodded and started thinking about my sister and my mum. After that everything the detective and the solicitor said just faded away.

I looked down at my feet and I wished with everything I had that I'd never found the gun.

Our books are tested
for children and young people by
children and young people.

Thanks to everyone who consulted on
a manuscript for their time and effort in
helping us to make our books better
for our readers.

*Also by **Bali Rai** ...*

Harvey and his family have the neighbour from hell. Mick is bad-tempered, rude and racist. His only friend seems to be his smelly, mangy dog Nelson.

But Harvey's always wanted a dog. And so, when Mick ends up in hospital, Harvey is the obvious choice to look after the mutt.

As Harvey gets to know Mick a bit better, he starts to wonder if there might be more to his story than first meets the eye ... But can an old dog really learn new tricks?

While Baljit shovels chips in his dad's chippy, he dreams of football stardom. Then the chance of a life-time comes along – a trial for the Premier League.

But Baljit is sure his parents will disapprove, and so the lies begin. Will Baljit's parents cost him his dream – or will his own lies trip him up?

www.barringtonstoke.co.uk